THIS BOOK BELONGS TO: Kenji

Merry Christmas 2017!

Grandpa Larry

merry Christmas
Kenji! I saw this
book a few months
ago in a bookstore
in San Francisco
and it reminded me of
your grandpa/ my dad!
we thought you should
have it and we can't
wait to read it to you!
　　　　Love,
　　♡ Auntie Elspeth
　　　　2017

賢光君

すてきな おはなしですね。

大きくなったら、きっと

好きに なりますよ。

　　　　おばあちゃる

LARRY AND THE
MUSTACHE

FIRST EDITION

Once upon a time...

A little boy was born.
His parents named him Larry.

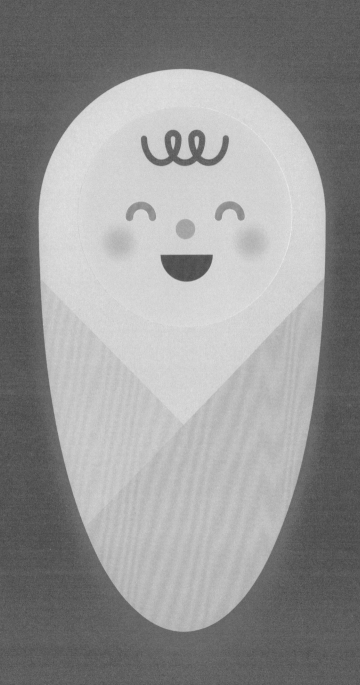

When Larry was only a few months old,
something strange appeared on his upper lip.

The next morning, there was
something even stranger on Larry's face.

And the morning after that, he had sprouted an ENORMOUS RED MUSTACHE!

The mustache would grow so fast that Larry could be a new character everyday.

"The COMMISSIONER"

"SGT. PEPPER"

"HARLEY"

"FREEDOM FRIES"

"The STANDARD"

"DUTCH UNCLE"

Before long, it was time for
Larry to begin his first day of school.

As soon as Larry got on the bus,
the other kids could tell he was different.

WALRUS!

WEIRDO!

HAHA!

No one would be Larry's friend at school.

But one day, he heard someone shout,
"HEY... is that thing real!?"

"OUCH!"

Then she jumped up and yelled,
"You can't play that alone mustache kid!"

From then on, Gracie and Larry
did everything together.

They were best friends.

Until one day, Gracie's father got a new job
and her family moved far away.

But by then, Larry was older and the other boys at school began to see him differently.

**Many years later, Larry saw
someone that looked very familiar.**

And from then on, they lived
HAPPILY EVER AFTER.

THIS BOOK MADE POSSIBLE
WITH THE SUPPORT OF:

Abdulrahman
M. ALSERKAL

Leslie & Troy
EILAND

Andrea
CEPALE

The
JOHNSON
FAMILY

Claire
DAVIS

Shay
OMETZ

Annelise
DRANGE

Carla
PETTY

Alexander
S. DUERRE

Susan
STEWART